A Fish Named Spot

by Jennifer P. Goldfinger

Little, Brown and Company

BOSTON NEW YORK LONDON

*To Michael, my husband and in-house editor, and to my big little
girls, Eva and Esme, for providing a healthy balance of
inspiration and distraction*

*Appreciation: My brainstorming partner, Mark, and Lois, for
putting me in the light*

First Edition

Library of Congress Cataloging-in-Publication Data
Goldfinger, Jennifer P.
  A fish named Spot / written and illustrated by Jennifer P. Goldfinger. — 1st ed.
    p.   cm.
  Summary: When he feeds his new pet fish dog biscuits, Simon's wish for a dog comes true in
a most unusual way.
  ISBN 0-316-32047-1
  [1. Fishes — Fiction.   2. Pets — Fiction.]   I. Title.
PZ7.G56495Fi 2001
[E] — dc21
                                                                                99-16411

10 9 8 7 6 5 4 3 2 1

TWP

Printed in Singapore

The illustrations for this book were done in gouache on smooth surface drawing Bristol.
The text was set in Simoncini Garamond, and the display type is Treehouse.

$\mathcal{S}$imon wanted a dog. He wanted a dog more than strawberry ice cream. He wanted a dog more than Christmas. But Simon couldn't have a dog.

Last year his aunt Loretta, who traveled far and wide and always brought back the best gifts, presented him with a puppy from England. But the fluffy dog made him itch and sneeze. It made his face swell up.

"I'm sorry, Simon," his mother had said. "Maybe another pet would be better."

Simon didn't even have a chance to name the puppy, and he felt sad that he couldn't have a dog.

One day the following spring, the front door flew open and in strode Aunt Loretta.

"*Jambo,* or 'greetings from Africa,' everyone; I'm here!" yelled Aunt Loretta.

"Crazy Aunt Loretta," thought Simon. "You never know if she's coming or going."

"Simon, I brought you this wonderful fish from Lake Tanganyika. On my way here I stopped at Barks and Bubbles pet store and picked up a tank and some things to go with it, but I completely forgot fish food. But don't worry — I fed the fish this morning, so it will be okay until tomorrow when you can get it more food."

"Thank you, Aunt Loretta," said Simon. "He is kind of cool-looking. I think I'll name him Spot. It's the name I had in mind for the dog last year, but . . . you know what happened."

That night, Spot settled into his new home. As Simon was getting ready for bed, he looked at Spot. Spot's fins looked a bit droopy. "I wonder if he is hungry," Simon thought as he scanned his room looking for something to feed Spot.

"Aha, here are some dog biscuits left over from last year. I'll get you some fish food tomorrow, but for now, these will have to do." Simon plopped them into the tank, *plop, plop, plop,* and went to bed.

The following morning Simon noticed Spot was much bigger.

That afternoon he was bigger still.

And that night he was even bigger!

Simon woke up the next morning bright and early and went straight to the fish tank. Spot was gone. Simon glanced around the room. Could Spot have jumped out of the tank? Would he be all dried out? Another pet gone. It wasn't fair. Then he saw a trail of water on the floor going under his bed.

As Simon knelt down to look, Spot scurried out from under the bed with a tennis ball in his mouth and dropped it at his feet. Then Spot flexed his fins, jumped up on Simon's bed, spun around three times, and plopped down.

"MOM!" screamed Simon.

When Simon's mom entered his room, her eyes grew wide.

"What is that fish doing on your bed? What's it doing out of the tank? Why is it acting like a dog? Where are my glasses? Get me a chair! Yikes!"

Simon laughed. "It must have been the dog biscuits I gave him."

Spot became Simon's best pal. Simon loved Spot. He taught Spot lots of tricks. Spot could blow bubbles, flip-flop, shake fins, even go for walks.

Sometimes they would go to the playground; Spot loved the slide.

One day, at the end of the winter, Spot and Simon were playing fetch by the frozen pond. Spot caught every throw, except one that Simon threw onto the pond by mistake. "Stay, Spot, I'll get it," commanded Simon. He went out onto the pond to get the ball. *Crack!* went the ice, and *splash!* went Simon.

"Help!" yelled Simon. Spot gave his tail a mighty wag and jumped into the freezing water. He grabbed Simon and fished him out.

They went home, and Simon took a long, hot bath.

The next day Spot started acting differently. He moped around the house and went to sleep next to the fish tank.

"What's wrong, Spot?" Simon pleaded. Spot just hung his fishy head.

"Is it the food?"

Spot shook his head and looked over at the tank.

"You want to go back into the fish tank?"

Spot wagged his fishy tail and licked Simon's face.

"Spot — now that you got back in the water you miss swimming around in your tank like a regular fish, don't you, boy?"

Spot was now too big for his tank, so Simon tried to find other ways to make him happy. On a warm day, he taught Spot how to turn on the garden hose and spray himself. He painted his room to look like a lake. He even tried fitting Spot in the washing machine, but Spot's tail got in the way.

The next day Spot decided to take matters into his own fins. . . .

Simon came home to a house almost completely filled with water.

He climbed a tree to look in his bedroom window. Inside, Spot was swimming happily through the room. Simon jumped into the water and swam around with him as the water continued to rise. "Wow, this really does feel like a lake, Spot!" exclaimed Simon. Simon and Spot chased each other joyfully from room to room. Simon came up for a breath every once in a while.

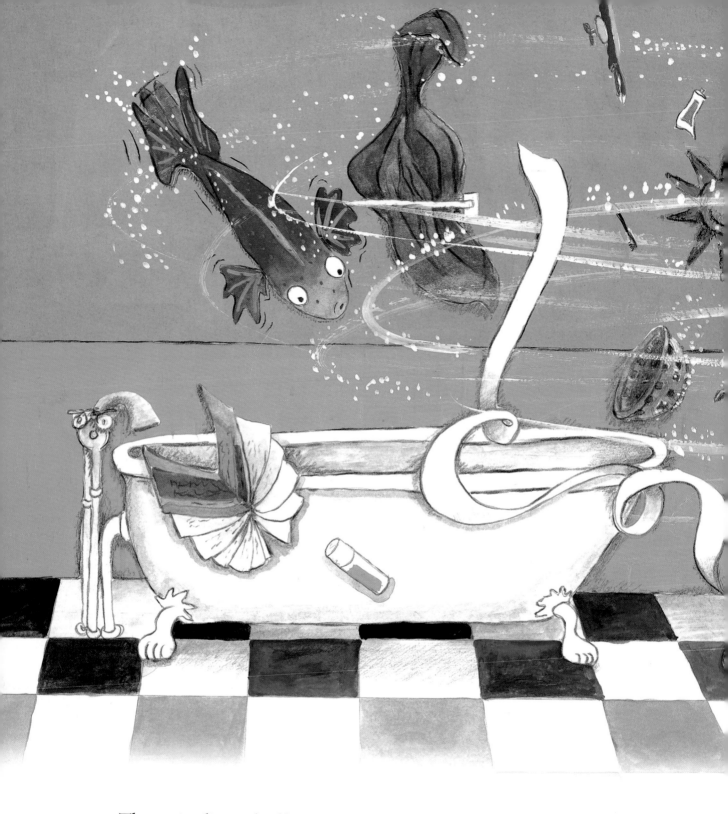

The pair slipped off into the bathroom and wound up all the bath toys. "What do you think would happen if we flushed the toilet, Spot?" asked Simon.

He pulled the handle. Suddenly they whirled and twirled in the cyclone they created.

They stopped in the study, where they found Simon's dad's instruments. Simon played the clarinet while Spot blew on the trumpet. They heard nothing but silence as they played. But bubbles filled with their music floated to the surface. Spot nudged Simon, and they swiftly swam to the fireplace and up the chimney.

Just as they reached the very top of the house, their music arrived to meet them. The notes pinged off the attic ceiling and flew out the windows. Simon laughed.

After listening to the watery concert for a while, the two friends realized they were hungry.

Next stop was the kitchen; Simon opened the refrigerator to bobbing fried chicken, pizza, and leftover desserts. Spot happily tasted

pizza for the first time while Simon opened the cupboard. Out floated pretzels, potato chips, and crackers in the shape of fish.

Simon had fish like them every day in his lunch box. "Try these," he mouthed. Without hesitation, Spot gobbled up several of the little fish crackers.

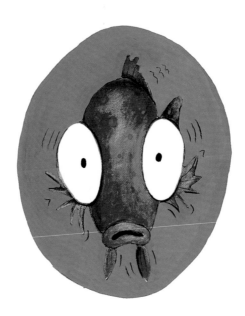

As soon as he had swallowed them, Spot's fins started quivering. Simon thought, "He's looking kind of . . . fishy!" Spot's eyes were huge and his tail wiggled wildly. Simon saw that Spot was getting smaller. It must have been the fish crackers that made him shrink again, Simon realized.

Simon didn't have much time to worry about Spot, though, because at that moment he looked out the kitchen window and saw his parents coming up the walk. *Click!* went the front door.

Suddenly there was a loud gurgling sound, and Simon and Spot
were sucked out of the kitchen, down the hall, and — *swoosh!*
splash! — out into the yard.

Sitting in the wet grass, Simon looked down at his feet and found a small Spot flopping happily around. He quickly scooped Spot up and put him in a puddle.

Once back in his tank, Spot swam contentedly. He could still blow bubbles, shake fins, and even go for walks.

At first Simon's mom was angry about the mess he had made, but now she is glad he has a pet that makes him happy. She says she even wants to invite Aunt Loretta over again — as soon as the sofa stops leaking.